A boy, a bug, and a bear want to fly a kite.

They take the kite outside.
The kite will not fly.
It falls to the ground.

CRASH!

It needs a tail.

"I will be the tail," says the bug.

The bug holds on to the kite.
Now it flies.

The wind takes the
kite high in the air.
The bug looks down.
The boy looks so little,
like a bug.

The kite
flies higher.
Now the bear
looks little,
like a bug.
"You look so
little," the bug
shouts, "like
bugs."

The wind dies.
The boy and the bear pull
the kite back to earth.
The bear looks bigger.
So does the boy.

"You don't look like bugs anymore,"
says the bug.
They all laugh.